Oma and Me
A Christmas Story

Written by Kevin M. Donovan
Illustrated by Mariana Dragomirova

ISBN 978-1-61225-238-4

Published by Mirror Publishing
Milwaukee, WI 53214

Printed in the USA.

For my endearing and ever entertaining

Shawn Michael

Oh Tannenbaum, Oh Tannenbaum,
Oma sings her song.
Christmas isn't here yet
but I can tell it won't be long.

She's taken out her candles,
four of them in a wreath,
and put them on the table
with my Santa plate underneath.

I'm thinking about presents.
I've been very good this year.
Oma lights the first candle,
then she pulls me near.

I'm hoping for a bike,
one that's fast and red.
Oma hands me some Stollen.
It's her homemade
Christmas bread.

Oma says the candles tell a story,
to give meaning to this season.
Toys and decorations are nice
but we celebrate for just one reason.
The first candle is all about "Hope"
and we pray for the people that need some.
We're lucky because we have each other
but some people are, "Oh, so einsam."

My hope is for Christmas presents.
I hope I get everything I asked for.
For the past few weeks,
I've been perfect.
I'll probably get even more.

The first candle night is over
when Oma and me sing a song.
We're supposed to sing Silent Night
but the words are all spelled wrong.

The next day we're making cookies.
This is where I help out.
She calls me, "Oma's kleiner Helfer."
That's what it's all about.

For Oma Christmas is special.
It has to be done right.
She says Weihnachten
is way too important
to celebrate in just one night.
So Oma or the Germans
invented a day that's neat.
I have to do a little work
but in the end I get a treat.

Dezember

6

Nicholas Tag

I clean my boots really good
and leave them outside my door.
In the morning, they're
filled with candy.
Who could ask for more!

I keep thinking about that bike
and all the presents I'll get.
Sometimes I drop little hints
to make sure she doesn't forget.

When the second candle night comes,
Oma has a story to tell.
I'm thinking of a new bike.
I hope it has a bell.

She calls the second candle "Bethlehem"
and her story is about a stranger.
A man brought his new wife home
but they had to sleep in a manger.
Then she talks about the Kristkind
born on Christmas night,
and the three wise men who finally made it.
"Ach, es war so weit!"

The second candle night is over.
Now I get to pick the song.
I can tell Oma
doesn't know this one
but she tries to sing along.

Frosty za coal man wiss a happy jelly bowl,,,

The days go by so fast,
singing, eating and cooking.
I don't dare search for presents.
Last year I got caught looking.

But I found my Christmas present.
I wasn't even trying.
It's just a winter coat.
I almost started crying.

The third candle night comes
and even though I'm just a little boy,
Oma lets me light the candle,
the candle she calls "Joy".

Joy is for all the people
who love life no matter what.
They're not sad for what they don't have.
They're happy for what they've got.

Oma's Christmas stories
make a little more sense each year.
Being nice and making others happy,
that's really real Christmas cheer.

Oma's lighting all the candles,
the fourth candle night is here.
I know there's a good story coming
so I sit in Oma's chair.

The fourth candle is for the Angels.
They watch over us every day.
We never ever see them
but they hear us when we pray.

Cookies, songs and Stollen,
I have everything I like.
Especially an Oma who loves me.
I don't need a fast red bike.

Oma and Me
A Christmas Story

What the German words mean

Ach, es war so weit! = Oh, it was so far!

Kristkind = Baby Jesus

Oh, so einsam. = Oh, so lonely.

Oh Tannenbaum, Oh Tannenbaum = Oh Christmas Tree, Oh Christmas Tree

Oma = Grandmother

Oma's kleiner Helfer = Grandmother's little helper

Stollen = traditional German Christmas bread

Weihnachten = Christmas

CPSIA information can be obtained
at www.ICGtesting.com
Printed in the USA
BVHW021623211120
593778BV00002B/5